Rifka Takes a Bow

To my parents, Israel Rosenberg and Vera Rozanko; my children, Susanna and Daniel and their spouses and their children.—*B.R.P.*

To Towa
—*C.K.*

Text copyright ©2013 by Betty Rosenberg Perlov
Illustrations copyright ©2013 Lerner Publishing Group

The images in this book are used with the permission of: The Granger Collection, New York, p. 32 (top); © Buyenlarge/Archive Photos/Getty Images, p. 32 (middle); Photos provided by the author, p. 32 (bottom both).

KAR-BEN Publishing
A division of Lerner Publishing Group, Inc.
241 First Avenue North
Minneapolis, MN 55401 USA
800-4KARBEN

For reading levels and more information, look up this title at www.lernerbooks.com.

Library of Congress Cataloging-in-Publication Data

Perlov, Betty Rosenberg.
     Rifka takes a bow / by Betty Rosenberg Perlov ; illustrated by Cosei Kawa.
        p.   cm.
     Summary: A young girl's family is part of a Yiddish theater performance group.
     ISBN: 978-0-7613-8127-3 (lib. bdg. : alk. paper)
     ISBN: 978-1-4677-1648-2 (eBook)
     [1. Theater, Yiddish—Fiction. 2. Jews—United States—Fiction.] I. Kawa, Cosei, illustrator. II. Title.
PZ7.P43247Ri 2013
[E]—dc23   2012028985

Manufactured in the United States of America

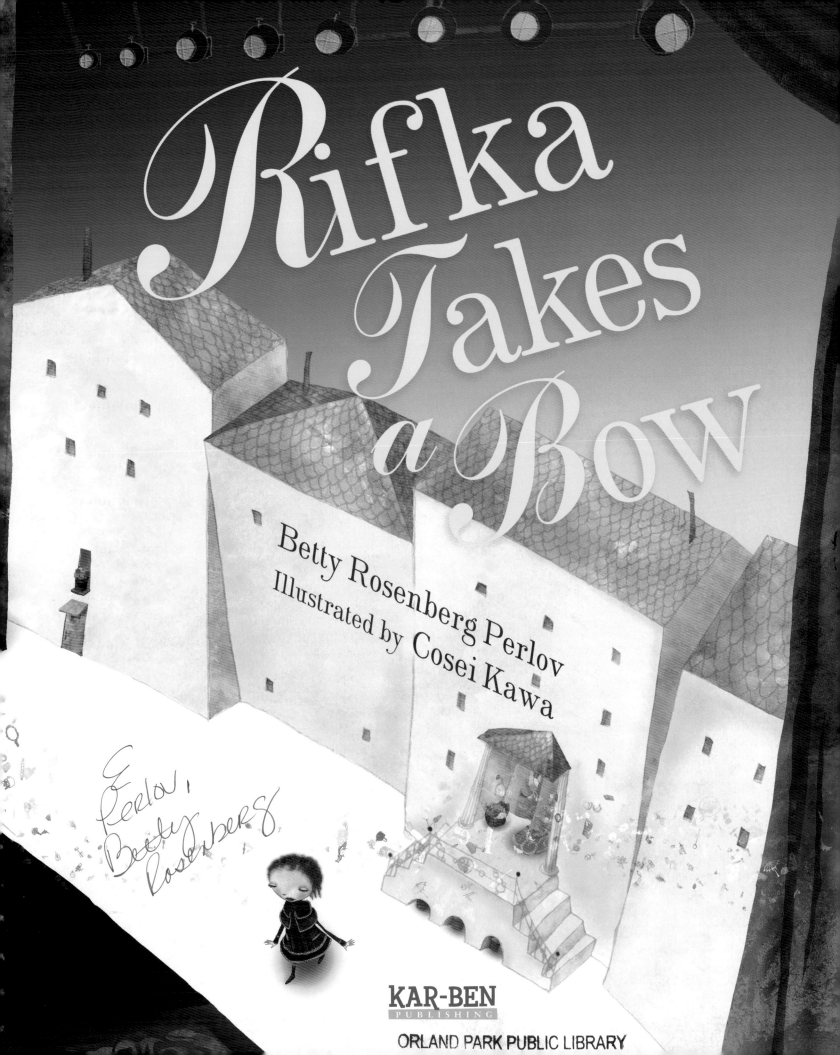

Rifka Takes a Bow

Betty Rosenberg Perlov
Illustrated by Cosei Kawa

KAR-BEN
PUBLISHING

P apa pastes on a brown, curly mustache and picks up a cane.
Mama puts on a white wig. She bends over when she walks.

Suddenly they are an old man and an old lady. I can
hardly recognize them.

Mama and Papa are actors in the Yiddish Theater.

Sometimes they take me with them to work. We ride the subway train in noisy, dark tunnels under the sidewalks. When we get off at Union Square we walk up a lot of steps to the street. I am always glad to see the sky.

On the way to the theater, we stop at the Automat for a snack. There are little boxes in the walls with glass windows that let you see the food. I always get cherry pie. I slide my nickel into the slot, and the window opens. After I take out my pie, someone behind the wall puts another piece there for the next customer.

Yiddish theaters line each side of Second Avenue. Mama and Papa
work at The Grand. When we arrive, first we go to their dressing rooms
backstage. This is where they put on their costumes and makeup.

Sometimes Mama dresses up like a little girl, with two long braids
tied with big red bows. One time she was supposed to be a boy, so
she put on short pants and pushed all her pretty hair into a cap.
She looked just like the boy who lives downstairs.

When I watch Papa put on makeup, he explains, "I take this little
piece of hair out of the package and pull it and pull it until it becomes thick.
Then I take this bottle of paste and brush it on my cheeks and chin.
When I put the hair over the paste, it becomes a beard and a mustache."

"Are you really my papa?" I ask him.

"Piff-Paff! Not to worry. I am really your papa. How else would I know your name is Rifkeleh?"

I like to visit the actresses in their dressing room. Each lady sits in front of a long shelf with mirrors and electric light bulbs. On the shelves are jars filled with powder and rouge, and rabbits' feet to puff it on their cheeks. There are colored sticks of shiny, red lipstick and blue and purple eye shadow. There are beads and ribbons hanging over the mirrors and pretty dresses hanging on racks. The actresses laugh and joke and tell each other not to say bad words in front of me. They give me candy and cough drops and spray their perfume on me.

Sometimes they let me wear their makeup.

It is very dark backstage when the curtain is closed. But you can peek through a little hole to see if there is a big audience. When the curtain opens, and the bright lights are turned on, the actors come on stage. Then the play begins!

Sometimes Papa takes my hand and we go exploring under the stage to examine the props. I am a little afraid because it is dark on the steps. "Piff-Paff! Not to worry!" Papa says. "I'll protect you. Come, Rifkeleh, Just look at these treasures. How about a crown with pearls? Some gold wine cups? A box filled with money? Here's a baby in a cradle. This doll must be thirty years old by now."

I see a king's throne, a garden gate, baskets filled with wax fruit, and shopping bags overflowing with presents. There are big chairs and little chairs. There's a table with a beautiful birthday cake. Papa says, "Don't try to taste it. It's made out of plaster."

Papa tests me. "So, tell me, Rifkeleh, when you see an actor with blood on his hand, what is it?"

"It's ketchup, Papa."

"When you see the actress drinking a lot of whiskey from the bottle, what is it?"

"Tea, Papa."

"When an actor hits another actor with a loud slap, is he hurt?"

"No, Papa, because a stagehand slaps his hands together behind the curtain."

"How about kissing?"

"The man holds the girl's head between his hands, and he kisses his thumbs."

When we hear the orchestra playing, Papa says it's time to go upstairs.

There are no lights backstage. I am very careful not to trip over the wires on the floor. Some of the actors are already talking to each other on the stage. There are bright lights shining on them, but the audience sits in the dark. Papa runs to get me a chair so I can watch while he and Mama sing and dance.

Today the stage is set up like the outside of a house, with steps going up to a porch. There are rocking chairs and boxes filled with red geraniums. I know they aren't real flowers. Pretty soon I get tired of sitting on the chair so I decide to climb up the steps.

Suddenly I am on the porch of the house in the middle of the stage!
The actors point their fingers at me. The orchestra stops, and I walk
over and smell the fake flowers so I will look like I belong. Papa sees
me and holds out his hand. "Come, Rifkeleh, come to me." I stand
between Papa and Mama. The audience begins to laugh, and a man in
the audience makes a loud whistle. Somebody in the first row yells,

I let go of Papa and Mama and walk to the middle of the
stage. "Piff-Paff!" I say in my bravest voice. "Not to worry."

I get a lot of applause, so I bow all the way down and blow
lots of kisses.

Piff-Paff! Not to worry. I am going to act on the stage when I grow up!

About the Yiddish Theater and the Author

Between the late 1800s and the early part of the 20th century, New York's Second Avenue was home to over a dozen Yiddish-language theaters that performed for the many Yiddish-speaking Jewish immigrants who lived in the nearby Lower East Side tenements. They presented plays on themes such as the conflict between Eastern European parents and their American-born children, and the tensions between Chasidic and "enlightened" Jews, and adapted works of Shakespeare and other world playwrights to give working class Jews a chance to partake of high culture. Many popular performers on Broadway and in movies and television, such as Molly Picon, Walter Matthau, and Sophie Tucker made their debuts in the Yiddish Theater.

Betty Rosenberg Perlov, 96, grew up in the Yiddish Theater, where her mother was an actress and her father a writer and producer. Always artistic, she was a "child star" on her father's weekly Yiddish radio soap opera. She grew up, married, and went to college late in in life, obtaining a Master's Degree. She has always worked hard to share her artistic vision; this book is her triumph. She lives in the Park Slope section of Brooklyn, New York.

Jacob P. Adler's Grand Theatre on Grand Street in the Bowery, New York, NY circa 1900.

A poster for a show from the 2nd Avenue Theatre circa 1900.

Betty Rosenberg, as a young girl with her mother, Vera Rozanko, circa 1919.

Betty Rosenberg Perlov, author of *Rifka Takes a Bow*, in 2012.